Storyteller Tales

Why Dogs Chase Cats...
and other animal stories

Why do dogs chase cats and cats chase mice? How did the kangaroo get such a long tail? And how did the mouse save the lion?

Find out in this book of traditional stories from around the world. These imaginative retellings bring animals of all kinds vividly to life and are full of action and fun.

Bob Hartman is a widely acclaimed author and storyteller. He is best known for *The Lion Storyteller Bible* and other books in the *Storyteller* series in which these tales were originally published.

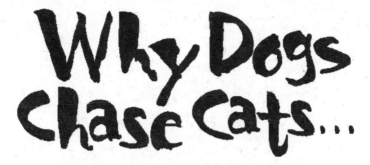

Why Dogs Chase Cats...

and other animal stories

Bob Hartman

Illustrations by
Brett Hudson

LION
Children's Books

Text copyright © 1998 and 2002 Bob Hartman
Illustrations copyright © 2004 Brett Hudson of GCI
This edition copyright © 2004 Lion Hudson

The moral rights of the author and illustrator
have been asserted

A Lion Children's book
an imprint of
Lion Hudson plc
Mayfield House, 256 Banbury Road,
Oxford OX2 7DH, England
www.lionhudson.com
ISBN 0 7459 4696 8

First edition 2004
10 9 8 7 6 5 4 3 2 1

Acknowledgments
These stories were first published in
The Lion Storyteller Bedtime Book and
The Lion Storyteller Book of Animal Tales

A catalogue record for this book is available
from the British Library

Typeset in 15/23 Baskerville MT Schlbk
Printed and bound in Great Britain
by Cox and Wyman Ltd, Reading

Contents

The Mouse and the Lion

The mouse skittered left.

The mouse skittered right.

The mouse skittered round a rock and under a leaf and past the dark, wide mouth of a cave.

And then the little mouse stopped.

Something had grabbed his tail.

The mouse wrinkled his nose and twitched his whiskers and turned around.

The something was a lion!

'You're not even a snack,' the lion yawned, as he picked up the mouse and dangled him over his mouth. 'But you'll be tasty, nonetheless.'

'I'm much more than a snack!' the little mouse squeaked. 'I'm brave and I'm clever

and I'm stronger than you think. And I'm sure that if you let me go I will be useful to you one day. Much more useful than a bit of bone and fur that you will gobble up and then forget.'

The lion roared with laughter, and the little mouse was blown about by his hot breath.

'Useful? To me?' the lion chuckled. 'I doubt it. But you are brave, I'll give you that. And cheeky, to boot. So I'll let you go. But watch your tail. I may not be so generous again.'

The mouse skittered left.

The mouse skittered right.

The mouse skittered away as quickly as he could, and disappeared into the woods.

Hardly a week had passed when the lion

wandered out of his cave in search of food.

The lion looked left.

The lion looked right.

But when the lion leaped forwards, he fell into a hunter's snare!

The ropes wrapped themselves around him. He was trapped.

Just then the little mouse came by.

'I told you I could be useful,' the little mouse squeaked. 'Now I shall prove it to you.'

The lion was in no mood for jokes. He could hear the hunter's footsteps. 'How?' he whispered. 'How can you help me now?'

'Be still,' said the mouse. 'And let me do my work.'

The mouse began to gnaw. And to nibble. And to chew. And soon the ropes were weak

enough for the lion to snap them with a
shrug of his powerful shoulders.

So, just as the hunter appeared in the
clearing, the lion leaped away into the forest,
with his new friend clinging to his curly
mane.

They returned to the cave as the sun fell
behind the hills.

'Thank you, my friend,' said the lion to the mouse. 'You are indeed clever and brave, and you have been more useful than I could ever have imagined. From now on, you have nothing to fear from me.'

The little mouse smiled.

Then he skittered left.

And he skittered right.

And he skittered off into the night.

The Monkeys and the Mangoes

Once upon a time, at the edge of a mighty river, a little monkey found a mango tree.

He munched on the mango and – Mmm! – it was amazing. Sweet and juicy and more delicious than anything he had ever tasted.

The little monkey crossed the river and took the mango to the Monkey King. When the Monkey King munched on the mango – Mmm! – he thought it was amazing too.

So the Monkey King, along with many more monkeys, made his way across the river to the mango tree.

The monkeys picked mangoes all morning and all afternoon, until it was night. Then they curled up in the branches of the mango tree and fell fast asleep. They had managed to eat many mangoes, but

there were many more mangoes left. As they slept, one of those mangoes dropped from its branch into the mighty river, and floated downstream to the kingdom of men.

The next morning, as the King of Men was bathing in the river, the mango floated by. The king had never seen a mango before, but he thought it looked quite tasty. So he picked it up and handed it to one of his servants.

'Eat this!' he commanded. 'Is it good? Is it bad? Is it poison? I need to know!'

So the servant munched on the mango and – Mmm! – it was amazing!

'The fruit is sweet and juicy!' he told the king. 'More delicious than anything I have ever eaten!'

So the King of Men took a bite and – Mmm! – he thought it was amazing too!

'Call my soldiers!' he commanded.

'We must travel up river and find more of this amazing fruit.'

So the King of Men, his servants and his soldiers made their way to the mango tree. When the Monkey King saw them coming, he led the rest of the monkeys into the highest branches of the mango tree and told them to keep very, very still.

The servants picked mangoes all morning

and all afternoon, and just as it was turning dark, one of the soldiers spotted the tail of the little monkey, hanging down from the highest branch. When he told the King of Men, the king just grinned.

'Roast monkey will go very nicely with this fruit,' he said. 'Take your bows and shoot the monkey down!'

Soon, arrows began to sail through the branches of the mango tree. The Monkey King knew that there was only one thing to do. He was the biggest monkey of them all, so he leaped from the branches of the mango tree, across the mighty river, to a tree on the other side. Then he tied a long vine around one of his legs and leaped back across the river. He hoped to make a vine bridge so the monkeys could escape. But the

vine was too short, and he could only make
the bridge reach by stretching out his own
body and holding onto the nearest mango
branch.

So the Monkey King, himself, was now
part of the bridge, and he called for the
monkeys to climb across his back to the
other side.

'There are too many of us!' cried the little

monkey. 'We will break your back!'

'Just do as I say!' commanded the
Monkey King.

So with the arrows flying all around, the
monkeys climbed across their king's back
to the safety of the farther shore.

The King of Men watched, amazed.
Then he ordered his soldiers to put down
their bows.

'Fetch me that monkey!' he commanded, pointing to the Monkey King. But by the time the soldiers carried him down, the Monkey King was almost dead. For, as the little monkey had worried, the weight of the rest of the monkeys had broken his back.

The King of Men held the Monkey King in his arms and asked him one simple question: 'Why? Why did you do it?'

The Monkey King's answer was more simple still.

'To save my people,' he whispered. 'For they are more important to me than any mango. More important than anything at all.'

Then the Monkey King closed his eyes and died.

The King of Men looked at his own

people – at his servants and at his soldiers. Then he ordered them to leave the mangoes and to follow him back to the kingdom of men. And there, in his own palace, the King of Men built a beautiful tomb for the Monkey King, so that he would never forget how a true king should act.

Three Months' Night

The pine trees stood tall. The mountains behind them stood taller still. And, in a clearing in the midst of the trees, the animals gathered together.

Their leader, the coyote, perched on a wide flat rock and howled, 'A-Woo,' so everyone could hear.

'My friends,' he called, 'we have a decision to make. Think hard. Take your time. And then tell me. How long should each day be?'

The animals looked at one another. They grunted and squealed and roared. Such a hard decision! Then they became quiet and set to thinking.

After a long while, the grizzly bear raised one fat, furry paw and slowly wiggled his four sharp claws.

'I think...' he yawned. 'I think that each day should be three months long. And the same with each night. That way...' he yawned again, 'we could get all the sleep we need.'

The animals were shocked by the bear's answer, and the grunting and squealing and roaring started all over again. But it was the chipmunk who spoke up most loudly.

'Don't be ridiculous!' he chattered. 'If I slept for three months, I would starve to death! I say we keep things just as they are – with one day followed by one night.'

The owl and the weasel and many of the other animals agreed. But the grizzly stood his ground, and soon the woods were filled with the noise of the animals' argument.

'Enough. A-Woo. Enough!' the coyote howled. 'We will settle this matter with a contest. Chipmunk, you must repeat over and over again the words "One day, one night" – for that is what you want.

'As for you, Grizzly Bear, you must say, "Three months' day, three months' night" over and over again – for that is what you want. And the first one to say the wrong thing will be the loser. Now clear your throats, take your places and let the contest begin!'

Chipmunk scurried up into the branches of a tall pine tree. Grizzly Bear settled himself on the ground and leaned against the trunk. And then they started.

'One day, one night, one day, one night,' the chipmunk chattered, faster and faster in his squeaky little voice.

'Three months' day, three months' night,'
the bear repeated slowly, but he was sleepy
and tired and found it hard to concentrate.

'One day, one night, one day, one night,
one day, one night,' the chipmunk chattered
faster than ever, and it was all the bear
could do to hear his own grizzly voice. And
that's when it happened. Instead of saying,
'Three months' day, three months' night',
the poor bear mumbled, 'One day, one
night.' And the contest was over!

'Chipmunk has won. A-Woo!' the coyote
howled. 'And so it shall be one day and one
night for evermore.'

But the grizzly bear refused to give in.
'I need three months' sleep,' he growled,
'and I intend to get it!'

He stood up and swung an angry paw

at Chipmunk. But
Chipmunk darted
away, so that the
bear's claws left
nothing but four
long scratches
down his back. Then the bear sulked away,
hid himself in a cave, and settled down for a
long winter's sleep.

And, to this day, every chipmunk bears
the marks of Grizzly's claws on his back.
And each winter every grizzly goes to sleep
for a three months' night.

How the Kangaroo Got Its Tail

There was a time when Kangaroo had no tail. Not a bushy tail. Not a waggly tail. And certainly not the long, strong tail he has today.

Kangaroo had no tail. But what he did have were plenty of children. So many children, in fact, that some of the other animals were jealous – particularly Bandicoot, who had no children at all.

One day, Bandicoot came to visit Kangaroo.

'Kangaroo,' he pleaded. 'You and your wife have six beautiful children, and I have none at all. Won't you give me three of your children to raise as my own?'

Kangaroo was shocked. 'No,' he said, as politely as he could. 'We love our children. We could never give them away.'

'Two, then,' begged Bandicoot. 'Just let me have two. I promise to be a good father.'

'No,' Kangaroo insisted. 'We want to raise our children ourselves, thank you very much.'

'How about one, then,' Bandicoot cried. 'Just one, and I will never bother you again.'

'No!' said Kangaroo firmly. 'We could not part with even one of our children!'

Bandicoot was angry now. 'All right,' he

shouted. 'If you will not give me any of your children, I will have to steal one!' And he rushed towards the baby kangaroos.

'Run, children!' Kangaroo hollered. 'Run away!'

The kangaroo children jumped from their mother's pouch and turned to run, but Bandicoot was too quick for them. He grabbed one of the little kangaroos from behind and held on tight.

Kangaroo was there in a second. He grabbed his child by the arms, and both he and Bandicoot began to pull.

They pulled and they pulled and they pulled. And then something strange happened.

The little kangaroo's bottom began to stretch – it grew longer and longer and longer!

'Help me, Wife!' Kangaroo called. So she began to pull as well. And the little kangaroo's bottom stretched longer still.

Finally, Kangaroo called for his other children, and when they began to pull, it was too much for Bandicoot. He let go with a sigh and ran away. And the kangaroos tumbled down in a pile of pouches and feet and fur.

'Is everyone all right?' asked Kangaroo.

'Yes,' said Mother Kangaroo.

'Yes,' said five little kangaroos.

But the last little kangaroo cried, 'Look!' And he waved his new, long tail.

His brothers and sisters began to laugh,
but when they saw how much better he
could run and jump, they soon wanted long
tails too.

And from that time to this very day, there
has never been a kangaroo without one!

Why Dogs Chase Cats and Cats Chase Mice

'Hear ye, hear ye!' said the king. 'I have a very important announcement to make. A dog saved my life yesterday, and so, from this moment on, all dogs are to be treated with the utmost respect.

'Food and water dishes must always be full.

'Toys and balls must be bright and bouncy.

'Playing fetch is now our national sport.

'And dog-catchers are officially unemployed!'

Then the king held up a large piece of paper.

'Here is my decree!' he announced. 'Signed with my name and sealed with my stamp. I am giving it to the dogs for safe keeping.'

'Woof, woof!' barked the dogs, as Dalmatian trotted forward to receive the paper. This was the happiest day of their lives. And they yipped and yapped and wagged their tails in celebration.

But when the day came to an end, the dogs were faced with a problem. Where should they keep that very important piece of paper? The dogs sniffed and scratched, barking out the best ideas they could think of.

'Dig a hole!' suggested Dachshund.

'And bury it!' added Beagle.

'It's not a bone!' sighed Spaniel. 'It's a piece of paper. The dirt will ruin it.'

'I know,' woofed Dalmatian, at last. 'Why don't we ask the cats to take care of it? They're clever – they'll know just what to do!'

'Excellent idea!' woofed the others in

reply, for in those days dogs and cats were great friends.

So the king's decree was given to the cats for safe keeping.

And they, too, held a meeting. They stretched and spat and cleaned their claws, miaowing out the best ideas they could think of.

'Climb a tree!' suggested Siamese.

'And hide it there!' added Tabby.

'But it's a piece of paper!' moaned Manx. 'The first gust of strong wind will blow it away!'

'I know!' purred Persian. 'Why don't we give it to the mice? They're very good at hiding things.'

'Excellent idea!' purred the others in reply, for in those days cats and mice were great friends too.

So the king's decree was given to the mice. And because hiding was, indeed, their speciality, there was no need for a meeting. The mice simply tucked the paper away in a safe, warm mouse hole.

And that would have been the end of the

 story, if one little mouse had not got a bad case of the nibbles.

He could have nibbled on a bit of carpet. He could

have nibbled on a bit of wood. He could have nibbled on a nice bit of cheese. But this little mouse chose, instead, to nibble on a nice bit of paper. And, sadly, the paper he nibbled on was the king's own decree.

He only nibbled a little at first. But once he'd started nibbling, he just had to go on and on. And the nibbling didn't stop until the paper had been nibbled clean away.

Unfortunately, it was at that very moment that a particularly nasty dog-catcher found his way into the kingdom. He picked up his net and climbed out of his wagon and set to work.

But the first dog he caught howled in protest.

'You can't do this to me! The king himself has forbidden it.'

'Really?' growled the dog-catcher.
'Then prove it!'

So the dogs went to the cats, and
the cats went to the mice. And when the
mice went to the mouse hole, all they
found was one fat little mouse with the
odd bit of paper clinging to his nibbling
teeth.

'Yow!' cried the cats, when the mice told
them the sad news.

'A-Woo!' howled the dogs, when they talked to the cats.

And no one was great friends with anyone any more.

So the cats chased the mice.

And the dogs chased the cats.

And the dog-catchers chased the dogs.

And, sadly, it has been that way ever since.

The Goats and the Hyena

Once upon a time, on a high and grassy hill, there lived three goats.

Siksik was the biggest.

Mikmik was almost as big.

And the smallest was Jureybon.

One day, the three goats went for a
walk through the rocky passes to a field
on the next hill. They grazed all day and,
as the sun began to set, they set off for
home.

Siksik led the way – for he was the
biggest.

Mikmik followed close behind – for he
was almost as big.

And little Jureybon straggled far behind –
for he was the smallest.

They squeezed past huge boulders and leaped over deep ravines. But as Siksik turned the very last corner, he found himself face to face with a very big and very hungry hyena!

'I have three questions for you, goat!' growled the hyena.

'Ask away, sir,' Siksik trembled.

'What are those points on your head?' the hyena asked.

'They are my horns, sir,' Siksik trembled.

'What is that patch on your back?'

'It is my woolly coat, sir.'

'Then why are you shivering?' the hyena roared.

'Because I am afraid that you will eat me, sir,' cried Siksik.

'For my dinner, I think!' the hyena

drooled. Then, with one blow of his paw,
he knocked Siksik down cold.

And, not a second later, Mikmik turned
the corner.

'I have three questions for you, goat!'
growled the hyena.

'Ask away, sir,' Mikmik trembled.

'What are those points on your head?'
the hyena asked.

'They are my horns, sir,' Mikmik
trembled.

'What is that patch on your back?'

'It is my woolly coat, sir.'

'Then why are you shivering?' the hyena
roared.

'Because I am afraid that you will eat
me, sir,' cried Mikmik.

'For my breakfast, I think!' the hyena
drooled. And, with one blow of his paw,
he knocked Mikmik out as well.

If Jureybon had been bigger, if Jureybon
had been faster, if Jureybon had not been
straggling behind, he too might have turned
the corner a second later.

But he was the smallest goat, and the

slowest — so he had time
to come up with a plan!
He hid around the
corner, so that the
hyena could not
see him. Then
he called out
in the deepest and angriest voice he could
muster: 'I have three questions for you,
hyena!'

The hyena was
confused. This was
his line!

'Ask away, sir,'
the hyena growled.

'What are these
points on my head?'
asked Jureybon.

The hyena was even more confused. 'Your horns?' he guessed.

'No, you fool!' roared Jureybon. 'These are my two sharp swords!'

'Second question. What is this patch on my back?' Jureybon continued.

The hyena did not like this one bit. 'Your woolly coat?' he trembled.

'Coat?' howled Jureybon. 'Don't be ridiculous. This is my mighty shield!'

Shield? wondered the hyena. Swords? And he grew more nervous still.

'And finally!' growled Jureybon. 'One last question. Why am I shivering?'

'Because you are afraid, sir?' the hyena shivered back.

'Because I am trembling with rage!!' roared Jureybon. 'And cannot wait to come round this corner and knock you out!'

The hyena couldn't wait either – to get away! He forgot all about his breakfast and his dinner and ran all the way back to his cave.

Then Jureybon danced happily round the corner. He woke up Siksik. He woke up Mikmik. And the three goats went back to their high and grassy hill.

Rabbit and Tiger Save the World

Tiger was huge! Tiger was fierce! Tiger had sharp claws, even sharper teeth, and beautiful orange-and-black striped skin. But, for all his good looks, Tiger was not very clever.

Rabbit, on the other hand, was small. And not very scary at all. Rabbit had long ears, a powder-puff tail and a brain that was every bit as quick as his long, strong legs.

Tiger wanted to eat Rabbit, more than anything else in the world!

And, more than anything else in the world, Rabbit did not want to be eaten!

One day, as Rabbit was out nibbling daisies for his dinner, Tiger surprised him. Tiger chased Rabbit through the jungle and across the fields and into a deep, rocky ravine.

There was no way out. Rabbit was trapped! So he stopped using his quick legs and used his quick brain instead. He threw himself, arms outstretched, against a huge boulder at the end of the ravine and waited for Tiger to catch up.

'Now I've got you!' Tiger roared. 'And I can almost taste the rabbit stew.'

'You may eat me if you like,' said Rabbit,

slowly, 'but first you will have to tear me away from this boulder I am holding up.'

'And what would be wrong with that?' asked the puzzled Tiger.

'Well, this boulder holds up the whole world,' answered Rabbit. 'I saw it start to roll away, and fortunately I was here to stop it. But if I move away from here, it will start rolling again – and take the whole world with it!'

'Oh dear!' said Tiger. 'I had no idea.'

'I'll tell you what,' grinned Rabbit. 'Why don't you hold it up for me and let me run and get some help.'

'Certainly,' said the worried Tiger. 'We don't want the world to roll away!'

So Rabbit ran. But he didn't run for help. He ran straight to his rabbit hidey-hole, laughing all the way – and safe at last.

The Four Friends

It was evening. The long, hot day was over. And the four friends gathered by the waterhole.

'Good evening to you all,' called Raven, high in the branches of a tree.

'I hope everyone is well,' chirped Rat, as he crawled out of his hole in the muddy bank.

'Very well, indeed,' yawned Turtle, as he floated lazily to the water's surface.

'And very happy to be among friends,' added Goat, as she bent down to take a drink.

The four friends talked and laughed and played by the water's edge. Then they went their separate ways for the night, promising to return the next evening.

But when the next evening came, someone was missing.

'Greetings, one and all,' called Raven, high in the branches of a tree.

'And how is everyone tonight?' chirped Rat, as he crawled out of his hole in the muddy bank.

'Very well, indeed,' yawned Turtle, as he floated lazily to the water's surface.

But when it was time for Goat to speak, Goat was not there!

'Perhaps she's late,' called Raven, flying down to join the others.

'Perhaps she's with her family,' suggested Rat, pacing back and forth in front of his hole.

'Perhaps she's met the Hunter!' cried Turtle, as he pulled his worried face deep into his shell.

'Well, if that's the case,' said Raven, 'I must go and look for her. We're four friends, right? And we have promised always to help each other.'

So off Raven flew, high above the jungle.

He looked left and he looked right.

He looked high and he looked low.

Finally he found what he was looking for – his friend Goat, trapped in the Hunter's net.

'Help me. Please help me!' Goat cried. 'The Hunter has gone off to check his other

nets, but when he returns he will kill me.'

Faster than he had ever flown before, Raven darted back to the waterhole.

'This may hurt a little,' he explained to Rat. 'I am going to pick you up with my claws and carry you to Goat. She is trapped in the Hunter's net and only your sharp teeth can set her free.'

So Raven grabbed Rat with his sharp claws and carried him over the trees to Goat.

Rat had never been so frightened. But
when he saw his poor friend, he forgot all
about his fear and set to gnawing through
the net.

Turtle, meanwhile, swam back and forth
impatiently across the waterhole.

'My friend is in trouble,' he muttered
to himself, 'and I must do what I can to
help.'

So he climbed out of the waterhole and
trundled slowly across the jungle floor in the
direction that Raven had flown.

'Hurry!' cried Raven, watching carefully
for the Hunter's return. 'He could be back
any minute!'

'I'm chewing as fast as I can,' mumbled
Rat through a mouthful of net. 'But these
ropes are strong.'

Raven watched.

Rat chewed.

Goat strained against the net and finally, with a SNAP, she was free!

Just then, there came a rustling noise from the bushes behind them. The three friends froze with fear!

'Hello, everyone,' puffed Turtle breathlessly. 'What can I do to help?'

'Turtle!' cried Raven. 'What are you doing here?'

'We've already set Goat free,' Rat explained. 'And now it's time for us to run.'

'But you are so slow,' moaned Goat. 'However will you get away?'

'We'll find out soon enough,' announced Raven, 'for here comes the Hunter!'

The Hunter burst through the undergrowth, and the four friends set off in all directions. Raven took to the air. Rat scurried under a log. Goat raced off across the jungle. But all poor Turtle could do was pull in his legs and hope that the Hunter would not see him.

The Hunter, however, had far better eyesight than that.

'The goat is gone!' he
sighed. 'But never mind,
here is a nice fat turtle,
just right for my dinner.'
And he picked up
Turtle and dropped
him into his hunter's
sack.

Raven watched
it all and flew off
to fetch Goat. He
whispered a plan in
her ear and, even before he had finished,
she agreed, 'I'll do it!'

Then, instead of running even farther
away from the Hunter, she ran right
towards him. He spotted her at once, and
the chase began.

Goat was too fast for him. Far too fast.
The Hunter threw down his big stick. He
threw off his coat. And at last he threw down
the sack that held Turtle – all to gain more
speed.

'I'll be back for you later!' he shouted.
And he hurried after Goat, who led him far
away from Turtle before making her escape.

Meanwhile Raven found Rat, and the
two of them chopped and chewed away at
the sack until there was a hole big enough
for Turtle to wriggle out.

The next evening, the four friends
gathered as usual at the waterhole.

'Good evening to you all!' called Raven,
high in the branches of a tree.

'And how is everyone,' chirped Rat, 'after
our great adventure?'

'Very well indeed,' yawned Turtle.
'Happy to be alive!'

'And happier than ever,' added Goat,
'to be among friends!'

A Note from the Author

As you may wish to read other versions of some of these traditional stories, I would like to acknowledge some of the sources I have referred to, although most of these stories can be found in several collections.

'The Monkeys and the Mangoes' from *The Jataka Tales*. 'Three Months' Night' from 'One Night, One Day' in *Tales of the Nimipoo* by E.B. Heady, World Publishing Co, New York. 'How the Kangaroo Got Its Tail' in *Djugurba: Tales from the Spirit Time*, Australian National University Press, Canberra. 'Why Dogs Chase Cats...' from *The Folktale Cat*, Frank de Caro, Barnes and Noble Books, New York, 1992. 'The Goats and the Hyena' from *Arab Folktales*, ed. Inea Bushnaq, Pantheon Books, New York, 1986. The 'Rabbit and Tiger' stories from *The Tiger and the Rabbit and Other Tales* by P. Belpre, J.B. Lippincott & Co. 'The Four Friends' from 'The Goat, the Raven, the Rat, and the Tortoise' in *Animal Folk Tales* by B. Kerr Wilson, Hamlyn Publishing Group, London.